KIAN

&

JC

DON'T TRY THIS AT HOME!

HARPER

An Imprint of HarperCollinsPublishers

WWW.EPICREADS.COM

LIBRARY OF CONGRESS CONTROL NUMBER: 2015961046
ISBN 978-0-06-243716-7
ISBN 978-0-06-256467-2 (SPECIAL EDITION)

16 17 18 19 20   PC/RRDW   10 9 8 7 6 5 4 3 2 1
❖
FIRST EDITION

TO THE ONES
WE LOVE
-KIAN LAWLEY

DEDICATED TO
THE ONES WHO
PUT UP WITH US
FOR SO LONG
-JC CAYLEN

CONT

ENTS

"LET'S START AT THE TOP."

OKAY, SO YOU PICKED UP THIS BOOK,

which means you want to know more about it. Or us. Or whatever. So welcome to *Kian and Jc: Don't Try This at Home!*, the greatest book ever written.

Let's start at the top here. We're going to take you step by step through it all, through our lives, growing up, meeting each other, getting in with O2L, O2L breaking up, launching our own YouTube channel, going on tour, being in movies, and pretty much making a living just by being our nutty, stupid selves. So, you may want to know why we called our book *Don't Try This at*

WE'RE PROFESSIONALLY TRAINED **IDIOTS.**

Home! That's easy. It's because what we do is dangerous. We've shot each other with paintball guns, electrocuted ourselves, and waxed our eyebrows off. We're professionally trained idiots. We can handle an ice bath challenge and not freeze our balls off. You might not be so lucky. So there's that and, uh, would you really want to read a book called, *Kian and Jc Talk about a Bunch of Stuff That Happened to Us in Our Lives and How We Got to Where We Are Today?* Right? We didn't think so. Also, there's no way all that would fit on the front of the book.

So, you're probably wondering why we wrote this book. We wondered why we should write a book too. So we sat down and tried to come up with a list of reasons why:

1. READING IS FUNDAMENTAL, YO! GOTTA READ SOMETHING, RIGHT?

2. WE HAVE SOME GOOD STORIES.

3. BECAUSE WE WANTED TO.

Yeah, so it's not the biggest list we've ever put together, but it got us to write this book, so . . .

WE HAVE

SOME **GOOD** STORIES.

Now you may be asking, who did we write this book for? Who's going to be reading it? That's the cool thing: It's a big party here, and everyone's invited. Moms, dads, kids, teachers, postal-delivery guys—everyone. As long as you can read, this book is for you—and even if you can't . . . we've got lots of pictures!

Okay, so how should you read this book? First of all, from the top of the page to the bottom. If you go the other way, it'll seem weird. But other than that, however you want to read it. If you're going to join the party, you need to be open-minded. Our book isn't like a regular book. It's a lot more real than most of the books you read, and it's a lot more fun. Oh, and you don't have to read it in order. You can start from the back. You can read every other chapter. You can even just look at the pictures. It's all cool. It's your book now. You can even cross out our names and put yours in there.

IF YOU'RE **GOING** TO JOIN THE PARTY, **YOU** NEED TO BE **OPEN-MINDED.**

So, that's about it. Go ahead and dive in, and by the time you're done, we hope you'll feel happy, get inspired, and know just a little more about us—or hey, **MAYBE YOU'LL JUST THINK WE'RE A COUPLE OF DUMB-ASSES.**

I WAS BORN AND RAISED IN SAN CLEMENTE, CALIFORNIA,

which is a town on the coast halfway between LA and San Diego. It's a pretty chill place: really sunny.

The earliest thing I can remember about my life was my first day of kindergarten. Man, I was so excited. My mom was like, "Okay, Kian, you're going to school!" and I said, "What's school?" (I had no idea what school was because I never went to preschool.)

So she walked me into my class, and I saw a bunch of kids and I was smiling and all like, "Oooh, new friends! A playground! This is gonna be awesome!" And then I turn around and found my mom had just . . . left. Suddenly I got all upset. Why was my mom leaving me?! I started crying. A lot. That's when I met my friend Colin. He was my only friend in kindergarten. He made me stop crying.

I have a great family: two sisters (one younger and one older) and two older brothers, and I always got along with them really well. Okay, well, I did argue with my sisters a lot—it's the thing you do with family, but I always looked up to my brothers.

And I've always been really, really close to my parents. My mom has always been my rock. Ever since the beginning, she's been there for me and my family. She's the one who taught me how to blow a bubble and how to snap my fingers. Ha-ha.

She also loves to cook, so there would always be a home-cooked meal that she prepared—but I'd never eat any of it because I'm a really picky eater. My mom would also always help me with my homework, since I was never really good in school. I have so many memories of us sitting at the table, spending countless hours—even staying up all night—trying to get my homework done.

My dad hardly ever helped with my homework. But we would do other stuff together. My dad and I would go out deep-sea fishing together a lot. Fishing is one of those sports that can be kind of boring for long stretches of time. You're basically

09/01/200

out in the middle of the water and just sort of bobbing around. Hours can go by and nothing happens. But the waiting is also kind of the fun of it. Not only does it give you a cool excuse just to hang, but when the big one finally bites . . . man, it feels awesome. And whenever I went out with my dad, he would always end up catching something big—like tuna or sharks.

YOU'RE BASICALLY OUT IN THE MIDDLE OF THE WATER AND JUST SORT OF BOBBING AROUND.

I remember this one day in particular when we were out on the water, bobbing around, and all of a sudden my dad's fishing line starts pulling like crazy! My dad calls me over and lets me reel in what he caught: an eighty-pound shark! That thing was huge! He had this big collection of jaws and teeth from all the sharks he'd ever caught—ten or twenty of them, hung all over the walls of his garage—and I thought it was so cool that I finally had my own set of shark jaws too.

AS FAR BACK AS I CAN REMEMBER, I WAS ALWAYS TRYING TO BE FUNNY.

The funny thing is, I hate eating fish. I mean, I really hate eating fish. Except for smoked shark and those gummy Swedish Fish. Those are the only fish I'll eat.

As far back as I can remember, I was always trying to be funny. I remember when I was around five or six and my sister would have these birthday parties, I'd always be making her friends laugh by making faces, tripping myself, falling down . . . stupid stuff like that. I thought there might be a less painful way of making people laugh. That's when I started learning how to tell jokes.

WHAT DO YOU CALL A FISH WITHOUT AN EYE?

Around that time, I started going to a Boys & Girls Club after school, and they had all these different activities for us kids: arts and crafts, gym, whatever. And one of the activities they offered was a comedy class. That's where I learned my first joke: "What do you call a fish without an eye? A fsh!"

In school I was totally the class clown. You know—the one who was cracking the jokes and doing stupid stuff just to get a laugh. I remember this one prank I played with my friend Jesse. What we'd do is, before class, Jesse and I would each take a huge mouthful of water from the drinking fountain. The goal was to see who could hold his water the longest. Every so often we'd look at each other and spit out some water to prove that we still hadn't swallowed it. If the teacher asked me a question, I'd have to try to answer with my mouth closed and get in trouble or swallow the water and lose the game. I was always doing dumb stuff like that. I never focused! My mind was always

A FSH!!!!!

I WOULD HAVE BEEN VOTED "MOST LIKELY TO BE THROWN OFF THE ROOF BY THE PRINCIPAL."

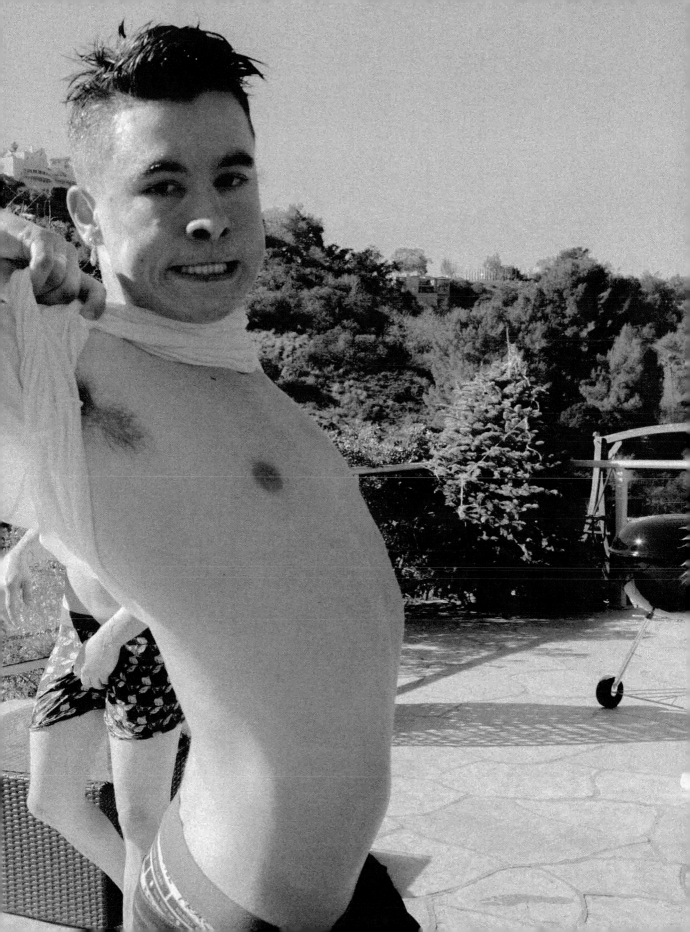

I KEPT GETTING INTO TROUBLE BECAUSE I WAS ALWAYS TRYING TO CRACK MYSELF UP.

somewhere else. And I kept getting into trouble because I was always trying to crack myself up.

My parents divorced when I was about eight. After that I got really rebellious. I was always in trouble. In fourth grade, I pretty much never got to go out at recess. The teacher always made me sit on the blue dot—this space by the back wall where she sent kids who got into trouble. I swear, I sat on that freaking blue dot every single day!

I remember in seventh grade there was this one girl who would always pick on me. She was just plain mean. So I'd kick her under the table whenever I could, to try to get her to back off. One day I waited until the teacher was looking at us, and I kicked her really hard. She jumped up and screamed some words she wasn't supposed to know, and got into trouble. . . . But then the teacher found out what I did, and I wound up getting busted for it. I probably spent as much time in the principal's office or in detention or being suspended as I did in class. Like I said before, I didn't like school—and school didn't like me back! I'm pretty sure if you took a vote, you'd find that I was the kid most hated by the teachers. I would have been voted "most likely to be thrown off the roof by the principal."

I dropped out of high school in my senior year, just as my sister was starting. All the teachers were like, "Lawley? As in, your brother is Kian Lawley? We're going to have to keep a close eye on you." Luckily, she was really smart and a good student. She redeemed the family name. The funny thing is that even though all the teachers hated me in school, when I go back to visit them now, they all love me. Weird, huh?

I DIDN'T LIKE SCHOOL—
AND SCHOOL DIDN'T
LIKE ME BACK!

Honestly, I was such a bad kid, I even got kicked out of the Boys & Girls Club! There was this big welcome banner that said something like, *Welcome to the Boys & Girls Club*. I told my friends to get the banner, and I'd put it in front of the cubbies where everybody kept their backpacks. Then I'd go through the other kids' stuff and steal their food. Hey, I warned you: I was a horrible kid! (I feel so bad about that one that when I tell that story, I usually just say I moved the sign in front of the cubbies

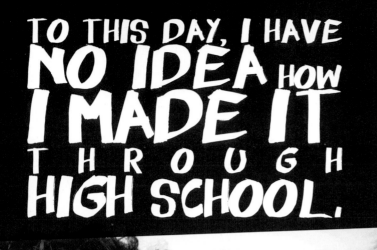

TO THIS DAY, I HAVE **NO IDEA** HOW **I MADE IT** THROUGH HIGH SCHOOL.

and threw their backpacks around. This is our secret now. So don't tell anyone, or I'll come to your house and steal your lunch.)

No surprise, but I failed almost half the classes I ever took in high school. My grades were so bad that my mom would cry if I got a C. And not a sad cry, not those I'm-so-disappointed-in-you tears. A happy, joyful jump-around-the-house cry. I mean, I pretty much got Cs, Ds, and Fs (except in PE and, weirdly, science. I did okay in PE and science).

That being said, I wasn't without my tricks. In English, when it came to writing essays, when the teachers would give instructions like, "Your essay has to be twelve-point font, single spacing," I would be like, "Okay, I'll do thirteen font, one-point-five spacing." No one was checking closely—and I hated writing. (Except, of course, this book. Which is superfun to write because I have an editor to fix my grammar, and there's lots of cool pics in it—like this one. In school they don't let you put in pictures, even though a picture is worth a thousand words. I mean, for most of my essays I should have been able to get away with two pictures and a title. But, nah, it always had to be twelve-point font and actual words.) I'd also do anything to get out of class. Whenever the teacher asked the class if anyone could run something down to the office, I'd be the first one to volunteer. I burned through all my bathroom passes in the first week, and I would have to beg my friends to give me theirs. Man, I couldn't wait to get out of school.

Even though I couldn't wait to get out of school, I did do one good thing while I was there. I had these two friends who I always ate lunch with, and one day we noticed this kid who always ate lunch alone at the back of the cafeteria. So we decided to eat lunch with him. Two weeks go by, and my friends got tired of sitting in the back of the cafeteria with this kid—but I stuck with him. Over time, people started to notice

him, and eventually he started to make his own friends. And soon enough, his friends are coming over to sit with us, and then suddenly he didn't need me to sit with him in the back of the cafeteria anymore. I didn't start out really trying to do something good. I just felt like this kid needed a friend. I sort of understood that. And I knew it wouldn't take much from me to help him out. I know it's a little thing, but I still think about it and feel like I put a little good into the world. I remember seeing him sitting at a lunch table full of other kids, and I felt like a momma bird watching her baby spread his wings. "Hell yeah, this kid has friends now!"

SO, I STARTED MAKING THESE SHORT VIDEOS.

Before there was even something called YouTube—or maybe just before I knew about YouTube—I was making videos. I started when I was about thirteen or fourteen.

So, I started making these short videos and uploading them onto Kidzbop.com. They were just me and my best friend, Sam Pottorff, playing around, or me dancing in the mirror or me slapping Sam—random stuff like that. Then I found out about YouTube, so I started watching a bunch of YouTubers. I figured, "If they can do that, I can do that"—and that was what got me into making videos for

YouTube. And back then YouTube was like one big family. No one knew what they were doing, and everyone helped everyone else out. We'd all get together on the collab channels and just toss around ideas and give each other advice. The cool thing is that some of my best friends are the guys I met on YouTube.

The first video I uploaded was one of me just making stupid noises and then speeding them up or slowing them down through my friend's computer. We were just screwing around, testing out different effects. It was completely ridiculous and sort of unwatchable, but that was the kind of stuff we uploaded back then.

I'll be honest: I uploaded a lot of weird stuff at first. My sister used to buy all these secondhand-store scarves, and she would ride on my back wearing all the crazy clothes she just bought—yeah, we filmed that.

About a year and a half later I started getting some viewers. I put a little bit more effort into my videos then. (We actually planned stuff before the camera was going!) At the same time, I started meeting a lot of other YouTube creators online, including Jc. We didn't meet in person until VidCon in 2012, but we were friends for a long time online before that.

When I found out I could be making money on YouTube, I applied for a Google Partnership. Basically Google was trying to make YouTube happen, so they were offering money to people to create content and get viewers. I applied, and I got denied. The problem was that I only had around a few thousand subscribers back then. If I was going to make real money, I had to get more viewers. And

I HAD MADE A **PROMISE** TO MY **MOM** THAT WHEN I GOT THE **FIRST CHECK** FROM **MY** FIRST **"REAL"** JOB, I'D **GIVE IT** TO HER.

that took a lot of work and forced me to post videos a lot more regularly. I had to start to take it seriously, funny as that may sound. Eventually I got my subscriber numbers up and applied again, and I finally got accepted. At the beginning it took a few months for me to make my first one hundred dollars—but I so remember when that first check showed up.

I had made a promise to my mom that when I got the first check from my first "real" job, I'd give it to her. That first check wound up being for 136 dollars. I know it's not, like, Bill Gates money, but at the time, to me, it felt like a lot. Especially since I made it doing what I love. And the best was that I kept my promise and gave her the whole thing. It wasn't about the money; it was about the respect. Tough as she's always been on me, my mom's also always stood by me and believed in me. This was my weird way of saying she was right. The money started coming in slowly at first: 100 dollars, then 110 dollars, 131 dollars, 142 dollars. Plus, since I was making my videos with Sam, we'd split the money. It wasn't much, but it was enough encouragement to keep me going. Mom and Dad still paid for most things anyway, but now I could buy some things for myself. Like what, you ask? Like candy. I bought a lot of candy.

Here's a true story: I never had a real job, but I did work at this drugstore once. I didn't get paid with an actual paycheck or anything. I got a twenty-five-dollar gift card to the store. And what did I buy with it? Hell yeah, twenty-five bucks' worth of candy!

My mom always told me that I needed to go to school to learn things and get a degree if I wanted to have a real future. My dad would say you don't have to go to school to follow your dreams. They were both right in a way. I always knew that school is where you have to go if you want to learn all the things you have to know to do

I ALREADY KNEW WHAT I WANTED TO DO.

the things you want to do. But I already knew what I wanted to do. So why spend all that time and money just to figure out that I should have been doing what I was already doing? In fact, school was getting in the way of me following my dreams. All that time in class and homework weren't helping me get ahead. So I decided to drop out of high school at the age of 17 and move to LA.

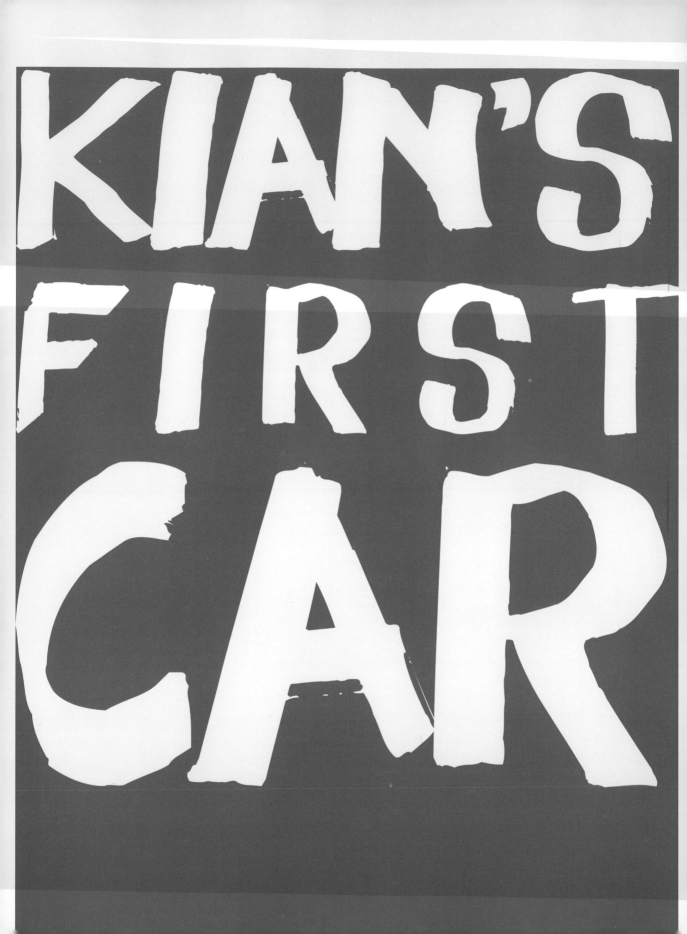

MY FIRST CAR WAS REALLY SPECIAL TO ME.

I'd just dropped out of high school, I had almost no money, and I needed a cheap way to get to LA and then to get around once I was there. I mean, I figured eventually I'd have chauffeurs and bodyguards and maybe even a butler—but at that point in my life, I could barely even afford a bus ticket and a candy bar.

Anyway, my first car was this black 2006 Ford Focus. I was in such a rush. I bought it the night before I was going to leave, and I couldn't really see it that well, so I just asked the dude who sold it to me if it ran and he said,

"Yeah." I bought it on the spot. No questions asked; no test drive needed.

I remember my mom was worried. She was all like, "You should wait until tomorrow when you can see it during the day," but I didn't care. I was too amped to go. I bought it, went inside my house, packed up all my stuff, and drove it up to LA the very next day.

I think what I loved most about that car was that I really didn't give a crap about it. I drove it like it was a tank. I'd park it with the wheels half on the curb. I'd hit trash cans by the side of the road. I never cleaned it out. With all the old burger wrappers and empty soda cans in it, you couldn't even see the floor mats. It was all dented, and one of the side mirrors broke off.

I BOUGHT IT ON THE SPOT.

NO QUESTIONS ASKED;

NO TEST DRIVE NEEDED.

Eventually I traded it in for my new car. (It couldn't have been that crappy, because I got a thousand dollars for it!) But I'll bet if I went back today, the dealer would still have it out on the lot. All you had to do was sit in it a minute, and no one would want that car.

Man, I miss that thing! It was the only thing I ever bought that I got way more out of than I ever would have expected. Maybe I should go buy it back. . . .

I WAS BORN IN HOUSTON, TEXAS, BUT I GREW UP IN SAN ANTONIO.

In fact, I lived with my parents until I was twenty. And when I finally left, I didn't just move out of the house, but completely out of the state. Sorry, Mom.

But I do have some great memories about my life at home. The earliest thing I can remember is the doctor pulling me out . . . and then I started crying. Just kidding. Actually, my first memory is my dad making me think he could talk to birds—and I totally believed him.

This is back when I was about four and we were hanging out in the pool and my dad was eating a bag of these Cheetos. There was this bird sitting on the fence near us, so then my dad looked at me and said, "Check it out, Justin. I can talk to birds." Then he starts making these bird noises like *teekle-teekle* (or, you know, some kind of

I was all like, "What did you say to him, Dad?" and my dad told me, "Oh, the bird said he was hungry, so I told him to come and get some Cheetos. Now he's going to go back to feed his babies." And I bought it. Then there was another bird that didn't come down to get the Cheeto my dad threw at him, and I asked my dad, "What did that bird say?" "Oh, that bird said he doesn't like Cheetos. He likes Doritos." I believed him for so long, and I actually bragged about it in school. Wow, I'm such a cool kid, huh? My dad could talk to birds.

I HAVE SO MANY MEMORIES FROM BACK WHEN I LIVED IN TEXAS.

I WAS A TOTAL MOMMA'S BOY. MY MOM DID ABSOLUTELY EVERYTHING FOR ME.

My parents divorced when I was six, and I've always lived with my mom, so I was really close to her side of the family. I was the oldest kid in our family—not just older than my brother and sisters, but all my cousins, too. Oh, and I was a total momma's boy. My mom did absolutely everything for me.

My mom's side of the family was really big, and back when I was about sixteen, we all started doing this really cool thing called Sunday Funday. Every Sunday my whole family would get together at my grandma and grandpa's house, and they'd both cook for everyone. Grandma would cook inside, and Grandpa would be outside, grilling.

At one of these Sunday Fundays I remember my grandpa once actually cooked two cow heads! He dug this seven-foot cooking pit and slow-cooked them for, like, three days. It was crazy for me to comprehend. The meat is called *barbacoa*. So we'd eat *barbacoa* all day, and then afterward we'd eat this dessert called *chongos*. (Which,

EVER SINCE I CAN REMEMBER, I'VE ALWAYS LOVED TO CRACK JOKES AND MAKE PEOPLE LAUGH.

you should know, is the best thing ever. It's like a snow cone flavored with pickle juice and topped with Tajín and *limón*. Awesome!)

So, at these things, everyone in my family was either adults—like twenty-five or older (hey, when you're sixteen, twenty-five is an adult!)—or they were little kids. The cool thing is that since there was no one my own age to hang out with, I got to have fun with everyone. If the adults were grilling or playing poker or bingo or whatever, I could hang with them, or I could go outside and play with the kids on the four-wheeler or trampolines. No matter what was going on, I never got bored. It was cool. I love my family.

My mom always said I got my sense of humor from my dad. He was a huge jokester—hey, he made me think he could speak bird, right? Ever since I can remember, I've always loved to crack jokes and make people laugh. My family knew me as the kid who would do anything. I was always just throwing it all out there.

Once I hit school, I tried to be the class clown, but only in classes where I had friends. You know that person who could just say anything in front of the whole class? I so wasn't that kid. If I didn't know anyone, I'd be the really, really shy, quiet guy. But if I knew people in the class, I'd be totally comfortable, cracking jokes all the time.

I never got in trouble though. Unlike Kian, I was a pretty good kid in school. I think the only time I ever got busted was for being tardy. My cousin Apryl used to play school with me even before I went to school. She taught me things and got me ready ahead of the rest of the class. So basically, it was really easy for me to go in and get good grades. Not to brag, but I didn't really have to try too hard. But then I'd get bored and mess around with friends and laugh. But I'd only do it up until the point where I could tell I was about to get in trouble, and then I'd stop.

I even wanted to make the teachers laugh.

(Not that I was a teacher's pet, but I always felt that life was just easier if I could be friends with my teachers. Easy extra credit—aayyee!)

I pretty much got straight As from kindergarten all the way through eighth grade. You could say I was a pretty average student mostly. And then high school started. . . .

And with high school came girls. I was a little playboy in high school. I was all about meeting girls and trying to get their numbers and doing cute stuff for them. I was that kid. I remember I used to text my crush during class and ask her, *Are you bored?* and she would be like, *Yeah*, so I would say, *Leave for the bathroom in ten minutes and meet me in this hallway*, or whatever. Then I would go to the bathroom too, and I would meet up with her just to talk about whatever—and then we'd both go back to class like nothing had happened.

I was a little hopeless romantic. I even learned to play guitar just to get this one supercute girl to go out with me. See, in my church youth group there was this kid named Anthony who played the guitar, and all the girls really liked him. So I was like, *I'm going to do that!*

So I got a guitar and learned a few chords and then taught myself a few songs off YouTube. Honestly, I wasn't very good, but I worked at it enough to know how to play a few songs. I knew this girl really liked the Goo Goo Dolls, so I learned how to play their song "Slide." Man, I remember practicing and practicing and practicing just so I could wow her. So one day after youth group, I went up to her and said, "There's something I want to show you. . . ." So I took her out to the church garden and played "Slide" for her. (I messed up a lot, but I got through it!) At the very end she was like, "Oh my God! That was so cute!" So I thought I had an opening, and I asked her to be my girlfriend—and she said, "No!" (Well,

I WAS A LITTLE HOPELESS ROMANTIC.

THERE'S SOMETHING I WANT TO SHOW YOU."

I JUST POSTED THE VIDEOS FOR FUN.

she actually said, "Oh, that's so sweet, but I don't think I should have a boyfriend right now, blah, blah, blah . . ." You know, that whole spiel.) After that, I pretty much said, "Screw the guitar," and that's when I discovered YouTube.

I first started watching YouTube when I found out about this guy named Mitchell Davis. He had this channel called LiveLavaLive, where he made these simple videos, like vlogs, where he'd do things like talk about getting a haircut. Man, he was funny as hell! He did this one video where he talks about this cologne he really likes and how it makes him feel like Usher. So he sprays it on, and suddenly all these effects start going off that make him look like he's in an Usher video—

then suddenly everything goes back to normal. Then he tries on another cologne, and everything goes all rock video around him. He really inspired me to want to make videos just like him. And, honestly, it didn't seem that impossible. I'd been making videos pretty much all my life. I'd always play around with our video camera when I was a kid, filming myself dancing or jumping into the pool or petting our cat or whatever. But it wasn't until January 1, 2010, that I posted my very first video to YouTube.

I started recording the video the day before, on New Year's Eve, using my MacBook Pro webcam. I was at one of my family's Sunday Fundays, and I just went around, filming things—like the fireworks, or my grandma drinking wine. I edited the whole thing together and basically just narrated what was going on: "Here's some fireworks"; then I'd show the fireworks. "Here's my drunk grandma"; then I'd show my grandma drinking her wine. I posted it on my very first YouTube channel, JcWithJelly, and boom, there was my first video.

I JUST WANTED TO BE MYSELF AND CRACK PEOPLE UP.

In the beginning my videos were pretty simple. Sometimes it was just me going to a park and recording the ducks getting fed, or close-ups of me feeding oats to horses out of my hand, or the light on the grass at sunrise. Oh, and the big thing was my Vans—I'd always be wearing Vans, and I'd make sure to show my shoes in whatever I was filming. Then I'd take all the footage and set it to a song I really liked, and that would be my video. Then I'd post it to Myspace or Facebook, and that's about it. It was really artsy stuff. But I don't know who would watch these things now, seriously.

I just posted the videos for fun. My friends and family would watch them, but that was about it. I did videos like that for about seven months, and then I decided to start over with a new channel. I wanted to be a bit more authentic—and funnier. I wasn't thinking about a career, really; I just wanted to be myself and crack people up. It wasn't until, like, my sixth video that I really "hit." It was called "Jc Caylen: Just Be, Yourself," and it was basically me saying who I was, what I did, and telling people to just be true to themselves. What happened was that Damon Fizzy (another YouTube creator) saw and liked my video, and he commented on it. Suddenly I was up from two hundred views to fifteen hundred views!

Like we said before, the YouTube creator community was a great place. It was like this big, crazy, awesome family. And when I was just starting out in 2011 and 2012, it helped so much to meet all these other creators who were also trying to figure it out. We'd watch each other's videos, comment on them, and get to be really good friends online—even if we lived across the country from one another. This is how Our2ndLife got started. This is how I met Kian, Connor Franta, Ricky Dillon, Trevor Moran, and Sam Pottorff—guys who would become a huge part of my life over the next few years.

JUST BE YOURSELF

But that was later. First, over the next year, I buckled down and started taking this video thing more seriously. I started a collab channel called CoolCollabBro, where I was collaborating with a bunch of other people, including Connor and Ricky. We'd do things like make videos where we were lip-synching to popular songs or whatever, so our channel would get lots of hits when someone would do a search for the real song because our video would pop up.

Around that time, like Kian said earlier, Google started something called the YouTube Partnership program. The idea here was that Google would partner with you to put ads up on your channel and you could make money. By late 2012 LifeWithJc had around twenty thousand to thirty thousand subscribers, and I got invited to join the program. I was so ecstatic when I got the letter—today anyone can become a partner, but back then, when it first came out, it was a big thing when you got to be a YouTube partner.

It turned out to be really hard to make money at it, though. At least it was for me at first. Google wouldn't send you a check until you had made at least 100 dollars, and it took me

I STILL REMEMBER WHEN I GOT THAT FIRST CHECK, I THOUGHT I WAS SO BADASS.

four months to make it to that point. But, man, I still remember when I got that first check. I thought I was so badass. Then I only had to wait another month and a half before I got another 100 dollars. Soon it got to the point where I was making 120 dollars a month. Then 180 dollars a month. But I still wasn't making a living creating YouTube videos.

Yet.

My channel really blew up in 2013, when I got a group of my eight closest friends (including my O2L buds, Kian, Ricky, Connor, and Sam), and we did a music video to "Call Me Maybe" by Carly Rae Jepsen. The song was already a big hit, and so when we put our video up on YouTube

and promoted it on Twitter, we were just thinking it would be awesome if Carly Rae saw it. But it turned out that Justin Bieber saw it and retweeted us, and since he had such a huge presence on social media, our video completely blew up. It got over half a million views, which was mind-blowingly *huge* for us then.

The funny thing was that Justin Bieber and *his* friends had just done a similar video of them all dancing around to that song—and that's where I got the idea to do one with my friends. I guess he thought it was cool that we did it too—plus, we were promoting Carly Rae's song, and he owns part of her record label. So it was a win-win for everyone!

At the same time I was working on my YouTube channels, I was going to college at UTSA (University of Texas at San Antonio), but honestly, being in college was the most depressing time of my life. My family didn't have a lot of money,

OUR VIDEO COMPLETELY BLEW UP. IT GOT OVER HALF A MILLION VIEWS, WHICH WAS MIND-BLOWINGLY HUGE FOR US THEN, so I had to work to pay my way through school by doing different part-time jobs.

My first job was at a Sonic drive-in, serving burgers and foot-long hot dogs on roller skates. (Yeah, I still have the videos—and no, I'm not going to post them!) I worked there for a good year or so. Then I worked at a frozen yogurt place called Spoon It, and then Urban Outfitters for about three months until I got fired because I blew off a shift to go to an Austin fan meet-up. Best decision I ever made!

Besides the crappy jobs, college just wasn't for me. I didn't have any friends, I had lots of early morning classes (which sucked because I'm not a morning person at all), and since nobody seemed to care if you showed up or not, I ended up skipping a ton of classes. I didn't do the homework, I'd miss exams—I just didn't care.

THE ONLY THING THAT KEPT ME SANE AND HAPPY WAS MAKING VIDEOS FOR MY YOUTUBE CHANNEL.

I started getting really depressed. I'd be working my ass off thirty hours a week at my jobs, getting paid $7.25 an hour, and then all my money would go to pay for school, which I hated and I was failing. I tried to explain it all to my mom, but she just didn't understand. I probably didn't really understand. It was a really bad cycle. The only thing that kept me sane and happy was making videos for my YouTube channel. All my friends were online, it was fun, and I didn't have to worry about paying bills, grades . . . whatever.

Once I started making enough money from YouTube that I thought I might be able to support myself off my videos, I made a huge decision: I dropped out of college and decided I was going to move out to LA.

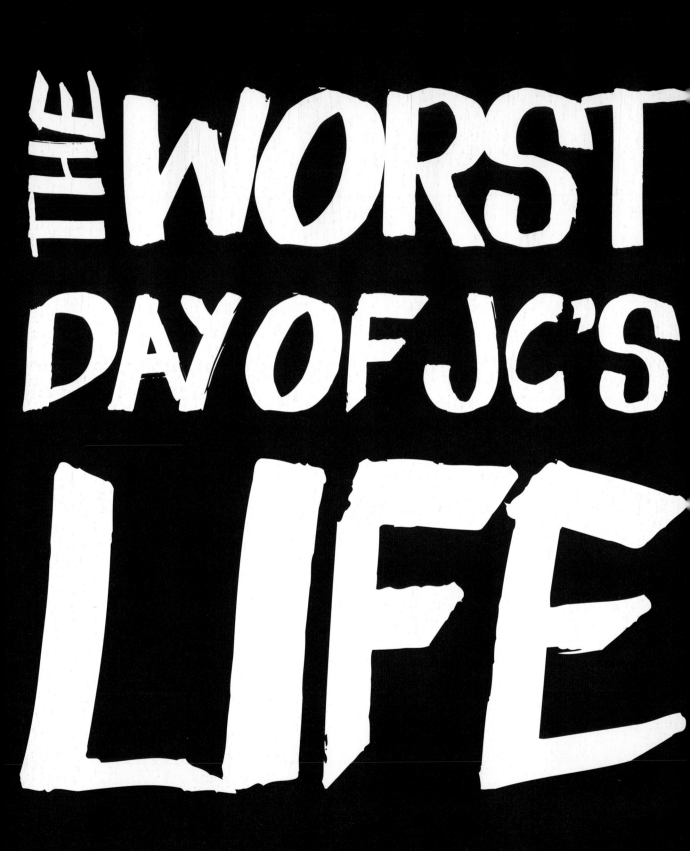

SO IF YOU WANT TO KNOW WHAT THE WORST DAY OF MY LIFE WAS,

I'll tell you—but the weird thing was that it was also the best day of my life. Yeah, I know, weird, but this is what happened.

When I was eighteen, I finally got my driver's license and my first car, an Infiniti G25—a totally badass car, by the way. I had this deal with my mom that if I showed her that I could handle having a car during the first week I had it, I could take it out alone on Saturday night. So, I was supercareful. I only drove my car back and forth to school during the week. She was impressed enough to let me take it out alone at night so long as I promised to be home by nine.

That Saturday I picked up all my friends, and we were having the best time—we went to the mall, we went to the park, whatever. So then eight o'clock rolls around, and I texted my mom that I was going to spend the night at my best friend's house. She told me that it was okay—as long as I had the car parked and was in his house by nine.

I agreed, of course, but I was totally lying. My friend didn't even get off work until ten thirty! We were really planning to go to this abandoned house to hang out. Me and my friends were having the best time riding around, blasting music, yelling out the window. . . . It was awesome. I was finally an adult! I had the night out with my new car—I felt so free! Like I said, it was one of the best days of my life!

But then all of a sudden . . . This red truck takes an illegal left turn in front of us, and I just broadsided him. I didn't even have time to release the gas; I plowed into this truck at full speed! I remember everything going black, and the next thing I knew, when I opened my eyes, there was candy everywhere. (We bought a ton of candy before

I STILL GET FREAKED OUT, THINKING ABOUT WHAT COULD HAVE HAPPENED. IT'S SCARY HOW QUICKLY EVERYTHING CAN CHANGE.

we went out that night.)

I stumbled out of the car. My leg was killing me; I was sure I'd broken it. (I didn't, luckily—just bruises.) My friends were still in the car, and we were all freaking out. I went over to the guy driving the truck and started yelling at him, but he was totally drunk, so he wasn't making any sense.

My car was absolutely totaled. When the cops showed up, they were amazed we all survived! One of my friends was bleeding profusely out of his head and had to be rushed to the hospital. I still get freaked out, thinking about what could have happened. It's scary how quickly everything can change. The whole thing happened in, like, the blink of an eye. And then I had to call my mom and tell her what happened. I thought she'd be pissed, but when my family got there, they were all just crying. It was such a close call. It could have so easily been so much worse. And then I started bawling. It was just a mess.

The end result was that I didn't have a car anymore because it was totaled, I was grounded for two months, and I had to ride the bus to school again. The whole thing just sucked.

So like I said, the best day of my life ended with the worst night of my life.

THE WHOLE THING JUST SUCKED.

WE MAKE
OUR MOVE

 **JC:** Okay, I know in the earlier section I totally made it sound like one day I just woke up and decided to leave San Antonio for LA, but there's a little more to the story than that. . . .

By 2012 I'd already been doing my channel for a while, and I'd become friends online with Trevor, Connor, Ricky, Sam, and Kian. That year we all decided to go and meet each other for the

I STILL REMEMBER THE FIRST TIME I MET KIAN.

first time at VidCon, which is this giant convention for YouTube creators. Okay, back in 2012 it wasn't giant—but it was still pretty big and awesome, and I had a great time while I was there. I still remember the first time I met Kian. He had all these ideas and was just dying to get started. We were all psyched to do more together—but Kian was out of his mind. It was awesome.

The best thing was that I finally got to see LA. And I totally fell in love with it—the weather, the lifestyle, seeing how people out here lived compared to back in Texas—everything. It was actually the little things out in California that I really loved.

Like when I visited Kian at his family's house in San Clemente; they would just leave the doors and windows wide open. I was all like, "Aren't you afraid of anyone stealing anything? You're not afraid of giant bugs coming in?" And they were like, "There aren't any giant bugs or people that

I JUST LOVE CALIFORNIA.

would just come into your house in California." And all I could think was, *Holy crap!* Then I saw that you could just skateboard anywhere out here, and I was totally in. I just love California.

I crashed with Ricky and Connor in their apartment in LA for two weeks, and then I made the decision to quit college and all my part-time jobs. I told my mom I was going to move to LA. It was crazy! I mean, yeah, most kids move out of their parents' house when they're ready to leave, but not a lot of them go halfway across the country just to go make funny videos with a couple of guys they

met online. It definitely wasn't easy for my parents to let me go. I think they were worried I was about to monumentally screw up my life. I was the one who got straight As all through school. I was the one who went to college. And so they always thought I was going to become a doctor or something like that, but in the end, I had to do what I had to do.

DON'T TRY THIS AT HOME! 91

I FIGURED THIS WOULD BE A **GOOD TIME TO MOVE** UP TO LA TOO.

KIAN: Connor and Ricky were already planning on coming out to LA, and they were going to pick up Jc in Texas on the way, so I figured this would be a good time to move up to LA too, so I could see what we could all do together. I mean, if they were going to be there in the same state, we might as well hang out together and see what happens.

Surprisingly, my mom was a lot more supportive about my decision to leave school and move to LA than I thought she would be. She knew I was making some money. She told me I could always go back and finish high school later. And college wasn't going anywhere. It would always be an option, and so I should go and do what I needed to do.

So the next day I bought my beloved piece-of-crap black Ford Focus with the YouTube money I'd saved. Then I packed up my stuff and moved out to LA. Saying it now makes it sound like it was an easy decision. It wasn't. I was freaked out, moving away and being on my own for the first time. But I felt like this could be something special, and I felt like I had to take the chance.

JC: SO WE ALL STAYED AT CONNOR AND RICKY'S APARTMENT IN WESTWOOD. FOUR GUYS IN A ONE-ROOM APARTMENT. YEAH.

KIAN: The apartment actually had three rooms: the kitchen, Connor and Ricky's room, and the living room. Jc and I crashed in the living room.

JC: I loved living in Westwood! I loved the nightlife. It was a college town, so there was always something going on. We used to ride our skateboards around and go see movies and

eat ice cream and just chill. We would hang out with Kian's girlfriend and her roommate. And in that little apartment we were all working on our channel and making, like, four videos a week, at least. It was a lot of work, but we were all supermotivated. We could see it happening in real time—more subscribers, more views. It just kept us wanting to do more.

KIAN: Oh yeah, that camera was always on!

JC: I remember the first time I really knew this was bigger than just a couple of guys goofing around in our apartment. I think it was 2012. I went to the mall. I think I was at the Apple Store, and two girls approached me and

"LET ME TAKE YOUR PICTURE TOO?"

wanted a picture. They knew me from the videos. They remembered stuff I'd done. It was awesome. A bit scary. But awesome. Then this mom in line was like, "Let me take your picture too?" She wrote my name down because she had no idea who I was, but maybe, she thought, her daughter would.

JC: SO WE STARTED DOING THIS THING FOR OUR FANS, where we'd tweet out where we'd be, and just have them come and meet up with us. One of the first big ones was when we were going to Taco Bell's headquarters. The Taco Bell peeps invited us to come try some new menu items they were testing. They asked us to see how many people we could get to a Taco Bell down the street. So, we were like, "Watch"—and we tweeted out that we were going to be at this one Taco Bell and to come by for a meet-up.

SOOOO MANY PEOPLE ENDED UP COMING OUT!

Sooooo many people ended up coming out! We had, like, a thousand girls outside this one Taco Bell. They had to call the cops to control the scene. It was awesome.

KIAN: Then we did one where we tweeted out that all the O2L guys were going to be at a park. We thought we might get a crowd, so we

BUT WE HAD, LIKE, A THOUSAND PEOPLE SHOW,

hired a security guard just to make sure everyone would be safe. But we had, like, a thousand people show. It was mayhem. We didn't think about permits or anything, either. We met everyone and hung for a couple of hours. But it was a bit out of control.

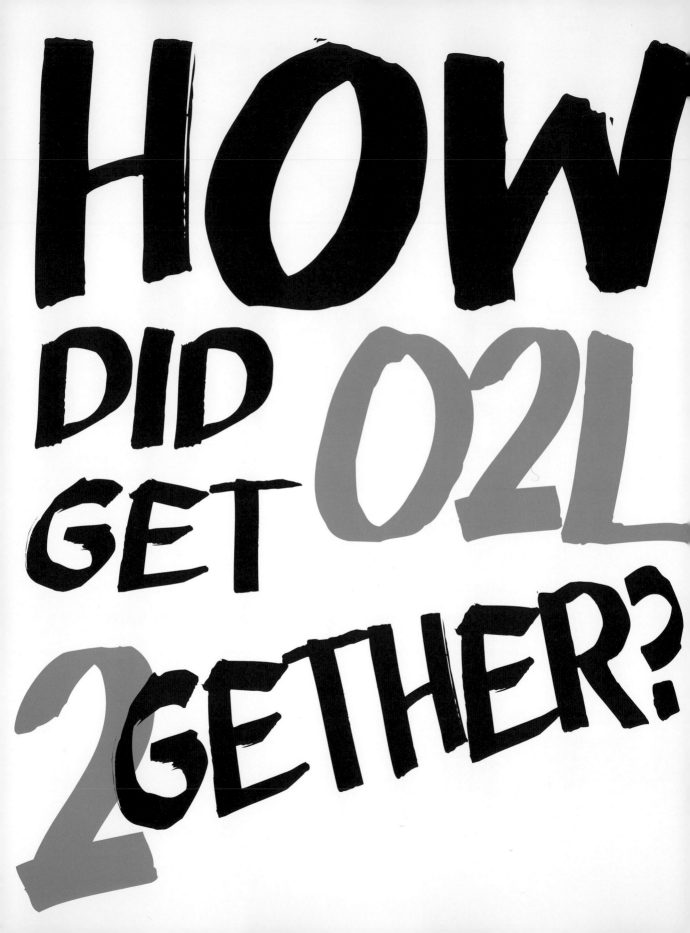

JC: WE WERE ALREADY FRIENDS, BUT WE ALL FIRST OFFICIALLY MET IN

2012 in Anaheim, California, at VidCon—the huge YouTube convention. This was about five months after we met online. It was our first VidCon, and we all just hung out together and totally hit it off.

I remember the first night there we all went to Sam's house, and I said, "Guys, we have to make a channel together! It would be so badass!" And everyone was in! So we spent the whole night thinking of names, icons, coordinating schedules—everything.

"GUYS, WE HAVE TO MAKE A CHANNEL TOGETHER! IT WOULD BE SO BADASS!"

Before we decided to call it Our2ndLife, we were going to name ourselves 99 Cent Collab.

KIAN: I'm 100 percent sure you were going to call it 99 Cent Collab because of the Arizona iced teas you were drinking, right?

JC: Definitely. We were all drinking Arizona iced tea, and on the can it said *99 cents*. Thank God Connor suggested something else! Actually, we were just going to go with Second Life, but that was already taken, so we settled on Our2ndLife, and eventually I started calling it O2L online (because it sounded cool and was shorter), and then everybody started copying me!

THEN THERE WAS THAT TIME WHEN KIAN WAS TAKEN BY GHOSTS

JC: ONE OF THE THINGS WE HAD TO GET USED TO WAS THAT AS WE GOT more and more subscribers, companies wanted to brand with us, to get us to promote their stuff on our videos.

KIAN: The two biggest ones were apps and movies. App makers would come to us and ask us to promote their new app, and movie studios would want us to talk about their new movies on our videos. It's not like we just sit there and say, *Hey, go out and watch this movie*. We'd also have to do stuff that had to do with the movie.

THE WHOLE THING ACTUALLY HAS A COOL STORY TO IT.

JC: There was one horror film we helped promote called *Ouija*. The studio flew us out to Chicago, where we got to be a part of a haunted house there. We filmed a bunch of videos—that was a totally fun experience.

KIAN: The whole thing actually has a cool story to it. It started in this one video, where I was playing with a Ouija board, and then suddenly I went missing from social media for a week. An evil spirit abducted me and took me to Chicago.

JC: So the idea was we all had to go to Chicago to "find him." Then they basically just filmed us walking around the haunted house until we found him. We also had a special meet-and-greet for fans at the house after it closed for the night. That was the best part.

WE ALSO HAD A SPECIAL
MEET-AND-GREET FOR FANS...
THAT WAS THE BEST PART.

JC: AFTER A FEW MONTHS OF LIVING IN THAT TINY APARTMENT IN WESTWOOD, we all decided to get a house together. Connor, Ricky, Kian, and I rented this four-bedroom place in Encino. It had a totally badass backyard. It was awesome living together. I'd wake up to Connor making coffee every morning. Ricky's room smelled like a sweaty farm all the time. Kian and I would play Mario Kart every day. We'd have friends constantly over for parties. I felt like I was living in LA. It was a really good year. Everything was booming.

JC AND I WERE **DEFINITELY** THE PRANKSTERS OF THE HOUSE.

KIAN: Jc and I were definitely the pranksters of the house. We were always messing with Ricky. We'd throw stuff like water balloons and plastic soda bottles at him from the balcony while he was lying out in the backyard. Oh, and one time we Saran-wrapped his car closed. He wasn't too happy about that. We pretty much made his life hell! We'd try to prank Connor, but he wouldn't react to it. It's only fun when the person freaks out—and Ricky would always freak out.

JC: One day Kian and I had a prank war just with each other. A whole day of getting each other back and forth. It started out small: Kian put shaving cream all over my mirror. Then I got him back by putting shaving cream all over his clothes. It ended with me dumping ketchup and mustard all over Kian's car.

KIAN: I also Saran-wrapped Jc's skateboard to a rock and threw it in the pool!

JC: We all had a really good time, which was a good thing, because we were all about to spend a whole lot more time together.

KIAN: You mean the tour?

JC: Yeah, I mean the tour, but I was trying to tease to that chapter!

WHEN I WAS YOUNGER, I WAS ALWAYS PULLING PRANKS.

The best one I ever pulled off was when I was still in high school. One day I really didn't want to go to my math class. Actually, I hated that class so much that I didn't want anybody to go. So I took this paper clip, jammed it into the door lock, and bent it until it broke off. We couldn't get into the room. They had to cancel class. And no one ever knew I did it. Well, until now. Sorry, Miss Woo!

But the biggest prank I tried to pull off but didn't get away with was when I was in the eighth grade. I'd been suspended for a week for trying to start a mosh pit at a school dance. So I was stuck at home with nothing to do, and I got bored. So, I went over to my friend Sam's house. I knew he'd be home since he was homeschooled. We grabbed some eggs from the fridge and went to my school in the middle of the day and just started egging the school. There was this one window that I knew was the principal's office. I couldn't resist throwing an egg at it. The problem was that there was a security camera next to the window that recorded everything! I got in so much trouble.

I GOT IN SO MUCH TROUBLE.

KIAN **SO ANYWAY, AFTER 02L HAD BEEN TOGETHER FOR ALMOST A YEAR,**

we had over a million subscribers. Things were starting to get seriously busy. We couldn't handle the business side and the creative side. We also needed some guidance to get us to the next stage in our careers. So we ended up signing on with a manager. At this point, we all decided to take things on the road and go on tour. It only took a couple of days to kick things into high gear. ROAD TRIP!

WE VISITED, LIKE, SEVENTEEN DIFFERENT STATES IN A MONTH.

JC: We visited, like, seventeen different states in a month. There was always a meet-and-greet before, then we had about an hour of downtime, and then we'd do the show.

KIAN: The shows were pretty awesome. There was a ton of interaction: we'd do improv with the audience, Trevor and Ricky sang, we'd do challenges where we'd bring audience members onstage, there'd be dance battles. . . .

JC: They were pretty big shows too. Usually one-thousand-people venues. Anyway . . . when I found out we were going on tour, I was pumped! It's one thing to do videos. It's another to actually get to meet the people who enjoy them. It was amazing seeing how many people were into what we were doing.

KIAN: It was all six of us—and Trevor's mom—in a tour bus. There were so many cool stories. . . .

JC: One time we were in Boston, Massachusetts, and the venue just sucked. There was no AC. It was just brutally hot, but the crowd was absolutely amazing! The first time we hit the stage, crowds will usually go crazy for maybe ten seconds, but this crowd cheered for, like, no joke, two minutes. They just kept going and it got louder and louder and we were all smiling. I completely teared up! That was one of the best tour dates we ever had!

BUT THIS CROWD CHEERED FOR LIKE, NO JOKE, TWO MINUTES

KIAN: I remember some bad times too. Like how we couldn't crap on the bus because the toilet didn't work right, and it stunk up the whole bus. So we literally pooped in bags and just threw them out the window!

JC: There would be some crazy times when girls would follow the bus for hours until we stopped at a gas station or something.

KIAN: In the middle of the tour, when we were at Penn State, I decided to dye my hair blue. Then Jc and everyone else dyed their hair different colors.

JC: Our fans thought it was pretty cool, and for the rest of the tour after that, fans would dye their hair to match their favorite O2L guy.

KIAN: Our biggest show was in New York, at DigiFest. They had all these different acts. There were, like, twenty thousand people in a stadium parking lot! That was amazing, doing our thing in front of so many people.

MOST EPIC ROAD TRIP OF ALL TIME.

JC: It was fantastic! All of it. It was seriously, like, the most epic road trip of all time. I got the chance to tour across the US in a tour bus with five of my best friends. It was a dream come true, and probably the best time of my life. But also it turned out to be a sad time, because what none of our fans knew was that O2L wasn't going to be around much longer. . . .

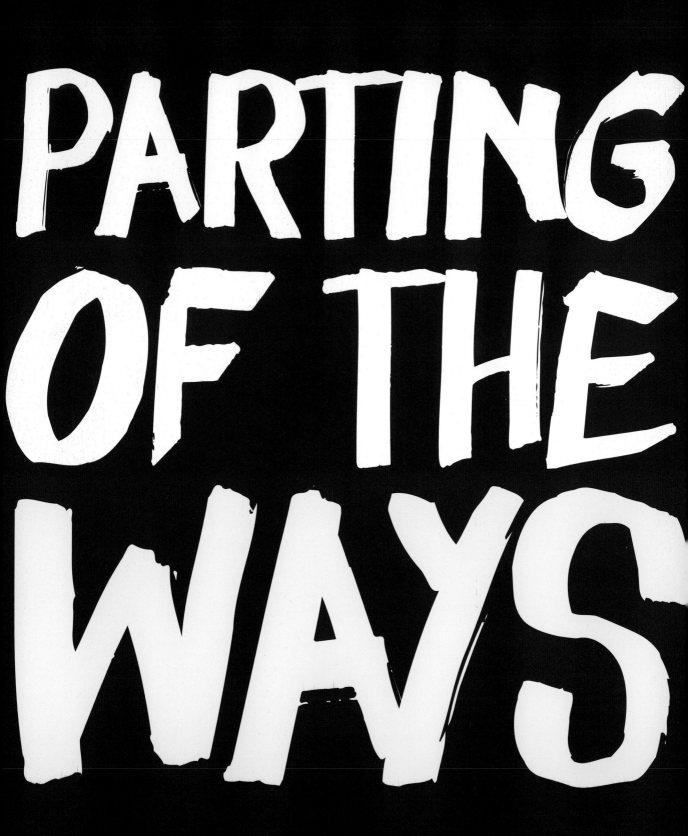

JC: **RIGHT BEFORE THE TOUR STARTED, CONNOR TOLD US HE'D BE LEAVING O2L.**

We didn't say anything to anyone on the road, but we felt sad, 'cause we knew it was all coming to an end.

KIAN: We knew no one could ever replace Connor. O2L was a brotherhood more than a channel. We couldn't replace any one of us and still be the same family, you know? So we were just planning on ending O2L altogether, but after going on the tour, seeing our fans and interacting with them, and having so much fun, the rest of us decided we wanted to see if there was some way to keep it going.

JC: We thought we'd revamp the channel, try collaborating with other creators, see if there was a way to make our videos better. But after about two months of trying, we all decided that it was time O2L ended.

KIAN: It was sad, but it was actually good for everyone. Now each of us would have time to do what he really wanted to do: Ricky and Trevor wanted to sing and Jc and I wanted to start our own channel. O2L would have just been a hassle getting in the way of each of us doing our own things. It was a hard decision, but looking back on it now, it was good we just decided to end it.

JC: We did a good-bye week for our last week together. We each made one last video, and then we made one final video with all of us in it together. We definitely tried to tell our fans that this wasn't good-bye, that none of us would be

BUT AFTER ABOUT **TWO MONTHS OF TRYING**, WE ALL DECIDED THAT IT WAS TIME **O2L ENDED.**

ENDING O2L WAS CRAZY HARD, BUT AT THE SAME TIME KIAN AND I HAD SOMETHING ELSE IN MIND.

vanishing off social media forever or anything. We wanted people to know this was a good thing for all of us and a decision we all came to together. We were still a family, but we were just growing up. The fan response was amazing. They totally got it, which, weirdly, made me even more sad to say good-bye.

KIAN: I'd been making videos with these guys for two and a half years. For me, to have to make one last video was really hard.

JC: Ending O2L was crazy hard, but at the same time Kian and I had something else in mind. . . .

JC: SO AFTER O2L BROKE UP AND CONNOR MOVED OUT, KIAN, RICKY, AND I wanted to move closer to Hollywood, so we moved into a three-bedroom house in the Hollywood Hills. We stayed in that place for five months, but it felt like forever.

KIAN: Our dog, Hazel, was a puppy when we moved in, and she ripped up all the furniture and chewed everything to shreds. Not to mention that she wasn't exactly housebroken. Nothing

WE THREW A PARTY FOR A FRIEND, AND SO MANY PEOPLE SHOWED UP.

was safe from her in that house. Oh, and we played Ping-Pong on this really big slab of granite in the kitchen and pretty much ruined it.

JC: Right after we moved in, we threw a party for a friend, and so many people showed up, somebody must have posted our address on Craigslist or something! There was even some kid who used to be on a Disney Channel show, sitting on our couch, acting like an idiot! We didn't even know him.

KIAN: That party completely cursed the house.

JC: The toilets didn't work. The pool heater didn't work. The roof would leak when it rained. . . .

KIAN: When Jc used the bathtub, the kitchen would flood. And then a few months later, when we thought nothing else could go wrong, two guys showed up at our front door, looking for the owner.

JC: We were outside the house, filming a video called "Musical Moods" for our new channel, and these two guys suddenly show up in front of the house. They get out of their car and start looking around like they own the place before they come up to us, wanting to know where the owner is. Apparently, he was in "big trouble."

KIAN: We told them we didn't know where he was, but they said that unless they got ahold of him, "things were gonna get ugly." These guys looked like those little Homies action figures come to life. Seriously, look up "bad guys" on Google images, and those were the guys who had come to our house!

JC: They finally left, and we started filming again, but twenty minutes later they came back, gave us their number, and said we should let them know if we see him anytime soon. That's when we decided it'd probably be a good idea if we found another place to live.

(THE YOUTUBE CHANNEL, NOT US, 'CAUSE YOU ALREADY KNOW WHO WE ARE...)

JC: Even before O2L broke up, Kian and I noticed that whenever we did videos together, they always had the most views. So we thought we'd make it a side project while we were still in O2L; a channel with just the two of us, called the Kian and Jc Channel. We knew that it was going to be difficult, making three videos a week for our new channel *and* a weekly video for O2L, but we were glad we'd started planning it when O2L decided to break up.

WE STARTED TO DROP HINTS...

KIAN: We actually came up with the idea of doing our own channel back in October 2014. We were planning on launching it in December, before our tour ended, but we didn't want people to think that our channel was the reason why O2L had ended, so we decided to put it off and launch it in January instead.

JC: We started to drop hints about it even before the breakup, a tweet here and there, but then finally in

January we actually did a seven-day countdown—each day was a different thirty-second video with us in different costumes. One day we'd be astronauts, the next we'd be dressed like greasers, then sailors, and each day we'd be counting down to the new channel's launch. Finally we launched on January 19.

KIAN: When O2L ended, we had something like 2.3 million subscribers, but with our new channel, we had to start all over from scratch.

WE WENT FROM NO SUBSCRIBERS IN JANUARY TO NEARLY TWO MILLION NOW.

JC: The response to the new channel was excitement. Once people saw that even though O2L had broken up and we were still doing our own things, the fans were cool with it. It wasn't like, *Oh, Kian and Jc broke up from O2L and wanted to go solo.* People started to get into it. And quickly, our channel became a hit on YouTube. We went from no subscribers in January to nearly two million now.

KIAN: Now it's a good thing that people are used to it. Everyone in the group had different aspirations, and O2L wasn't going to last forever, and now we're all getting to do our own thing. I think people respect that.

JC: Kian and I are just on the same wavelength about things. With O2L, we'd have to get six guys to agree; now there's just the two of us deciding what to do.

KIAN: The videos we do are more personal and straightforward. They're more direct and honest. It's not just the big things but the tone. The tone is the thing that's the most different.

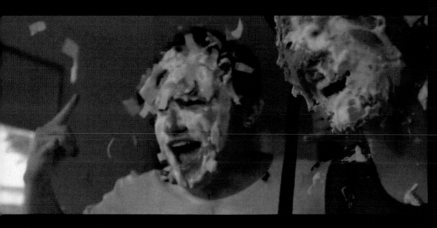

NALLY KISS!!! // Ask KianAndJc

To Do In A Hotel Room

To Do In A Hotel Room

156 KIAN & JC

JC: Our audience is more mature now. We don't have to bleep the bad words out, and the audience can get the sex jokes we make!

KIAN: It's not like we consciously try to put in extra sex jokes or swearing or whatever. It's just that with our new videos, we don't hold back. It's more true to who we are and what we think is funny. We didn't have a real vision going into this new channel, thinking, *Oh, we're gonna get more money, or have new, different fans* or anything like that. We were just going into it being ourselves, and we thought that whatever happens will happen. And the great thing is that the fans have really responded. Last I looked, we're at more than one hundred million views. The response has totally blown us away. We're making a living doing this—and that's just awesome.

JC: We're always looking to challenge ourselves, to see what's different, what's new. I don't want to ever get too comfortable. I want to push the boundaries and

WE'RE **ALWAYS** TRYING TO COME UP WITH **NEW IDEAS.**

constantly give our fans something they haven't seen before. And this is the vehicle for it. We're doing everything we ever wanted to—skits, short films, challenges, pranks, sit-down series, and vlogs—all sorts of things. We're not the first duo to ever do a channel, but we're always working to do things on it that no one has ever done.

KIAN: And we're going to bring more on the Kian and Jc Channel, stuff we haven't done before: things like outtakes, deleted scenes, bloopers, bonus content—we're always trying to come up with new ideas and create new content.

JC: We're always working on our videos. We have film days scheduled once a week with a film crew, but then we film ourselves over the weekend and on Monday, then we have the rest of the week to write and edit skits. We try to mix in the more produced stuff with the more down-and-dirty stuff. We just want to keep

pushing ourselves, trying new things, seeing what our fans react to. It's all one big experiment. People ask how we come up with our skits, and I always say we're just not afraid to try anything. There's no secret formula. We just put ourselves out there, we're real about it, and we deal with whatever comes.

KIAN: What changed the most after O2L was that when you're in a group of six people, you spend maybe one day filming, and then you have to wait a whole week until it's your turn again. Now we get to make videos at least twice a week.

JC: This is our baby. It's our lives. We spend all our time working on our channel. It means so much to us, and we really care about the quality of what we put out.

THE KIDS WHO WATCH YOUTUBE CAN SPOT A POSEUR FROM A MILE AWAY.

Middle Schoolers Try Alcohol - BLOOPERS

Egg Roulette Challenge - BLOOPERS

Kian usually gets cranky...

WE MOVED INTO A NEW HOUSE!!! // KianAndJc

KIAN: What pisses me off is when I see people on YouTube just doing stupid, boring stuff, like showing their abs or whatever, just so they can go around and brag. It's like, *Hey, dudes, I have fifteen thousand followers!* And then they move out to LA and try to make it here, and they can't, because they don't work at what they do. They think they can just throw anything up on YouTube and people will watch. Kids know what's crap and what isn't. People don't always get it, but the kids who watch YouTube can spot a poseur from a mile away.

KIAN: AFTER THAT RUN-IN WITH THE GANGSTAS, WE MOVED OUT OF THAT HOUSE PRETTY MUCH IMMEDIATELY.

JC: Even though we paid a year's rent up front! We tried to get our money back, but they told us that we did a hundred thousand dollars' worth of damage to the house—

KIAN: Which was pretty much true.

JC: So while we were looking for a new place to live, we spent the next four weeks living in four different hotels. We kept getting kicked out! The first hotel was a really nice, expensive place that

WE KEPT GETTING KICKED OUT!

turned out to be real sticklers about us keeping our rooms clean. We'd throw food wrappers on our floor and stuff, and after a few days they started hinting that we should leave.

KIAN: They just didn't make us feel welcome anymore.

JC: We got kicked out of the next hotel the same night we checked in. It was three in the morning when they booted us for being too loud. We had nowhere to go, so we had to crash with friends for the night. Then the third hotel we stayed at for a good week or so—

KIAN: Before we got kicked out again.

JC: We were filming a challenge video where

I DECIDED TO PUT ON THESE REALLY SHORT SHORTS.

the loser had to go down to the hotel lobby in his underwear and ask the first employee he saw to marry him.

KIAN: And I lost. But I didn't want to wear just my boxers, so I decided to put on these really short shorts.

JC: So while Kian was doing his thing, I was going to pants him, but I accidentally pulled his shorts too hard, and his underwear came down with them. He flashed his junk to the hotel employee.

KIAN: Technically, we didn't get kicked out, but when we tried to book rooms for the

4:26 / 5:35

WE WERE LIVING OUT OF OUR SUITCASES.

next week, they told us they were "sold out." I'm just sayin'. . . It was rough, trying to find a new home while we were staying at hotels. We had no kitchen. We had to live off of gas station food and hotel food. We were living out of our suitcases. And we were working. We were still making videos. Those four weeks sucked.

But then we finally found the house where we are now. And we love it! It's such a great place to film our stuff! We have a pool, pool table, lots of room for activities—everything a growing boy needs.

KIAN ONE OF THE CRAZIEST THINGS WE EVER DID WAS PLAY MARCO POLO PAINTBALL WITH THE JANOSKIANS.

We've been friends with them for a while. They do a lot of the same kinds of things we do—crazy challenges and stuff. So we wanted to bring our two worlds together and see what would happen.

JC: The paintball challenge was one of the craziest, most painful things I've ever done! We had one shooter who was blindfolded, and then the rest of us lined up against a wall, shirtless, and he said, "Marco," and we all had to say, "Polo," and then we got shot.

KIAN: I got hit six times! Once in the ass! Oh man, you know that feeling when you get hit in the ass so hard that you immediately want to throw up? I had to grab my butt cheeks and run away.

JC: I got shot seven or eight times. Getting shot with a paintball while you're shirtless frickin' hurts!

KIAN: What about a coin-toss Taser challenge?

JC: Huh? Who wants to do that?

KIAN: Me and you!

JC: No, we definitely never talked about doing that.

KIAN: You toss a coin, and see if it comes up heads or tails, and that says whether or not you get Tased.

JC: That does not sound fun at all.

KIAN: Okay, maybe not a Taser. Maybe a stun gun. Something that can shock the piss out of you!

We definitely do a lot more dangerous, painful stuff now with our new channel. Like when we do challenges with mousetraps and stuff. Yeah, it'll hurt for a little bit, but it goes away, and it's fun. Plus, I can take the pain better than Kian.

It's true: I scream a lot. People are always making comments like, *Oh, don't get hurt for our entertainment!* but those are the videos that do the damn best. The more it hurts, the more views we get. They're the ones that people secretly want us to do!

DISCLAIMER:
A MESSAGE FROM
KIAN AND JC

JC: We're professional idiots.
KIAN: So like the book title says, don't try this at home!

I LOVE TAKING ROAD TRIPS. I LOVE DRIVING. I LOVE GETTING TO SEE THE WORLD.

I love just being on the move. So I decided to document the latest trip I took by turning the whole thing into a seven-video series that I aired on my own personal YouTube channel.

I went on the trip with a few of my really close friends—Dom, Anthony, JJ, Louis, and Guigs. I chose each one because he has a special talent: we're filmmakers, graphic designers, daily bloggers, and YouTubers. It was a total dream team. Every one of us loved being on the road and loved traveling and experiencing things.

We decided to go up the West Coast and stop in San Francisco, Portland, Seattle, all the way up to Vancouver, and then hit Boise, Salt Lake City, Arches National Park, and wrap up in Vegas before heading home. We scheduled four meet-ups while we were traveling, and I'm being

IT WAS A TOTAL DREAM TEAM. EVERY ONE OF US LOVED BEING ON THE ROAD.

completely serious when I say we were late to every single one! It got progressively worse as we went: at the first stop we were three hours late; the second stop we were eight hours late; and by the time of the third stop, we were so late that we just had to skip it. (We were actually on time for our fourth scheduled stop, but only because we had canceled the third.)

At the first stop in Oregon, at Haystack Rock, we had a meet-up with, like, 150 people. Totally chill. So much fun. Louis actually caught a seagull. Don't ask me how. Of course, he let it go. No animals were harmed in the making of this—no worries.

Seattle was the craziest. We parked the RV in

a lot before we were going to head out to a meet-up, and there was this sketchy-looking guy there. We didn't think too much about it. But then when we got back, he was still there, and he came up to us and told us there was a bomb under our RV. We freaked. We had to call the cops. Turns out the guy was a little loco and had been

Catching Seagulls in Oregon // #7DaysOnTheRoad

telling people he was a bodyguard. So weird. There was no bomb, but it still really had us all freaked out. After that we started going toward Arches National Park in Utah, but on the way we stopped in Boise, Idaho—but didn't do anything there! Seriously, there were, like, maybe three fans in that whole town, so we met them at a skate park to say hey, and then we just kept on going.

It was awesome. It was just the greatest experience, driving around with my friends, meeting fans, and seeing a little bit of the ol' USA. After I'm done filming *Tagged*, this new TV series I'm working on, I can't wait to go out again.

ACTUALLY, THE IDEA OF MARRIAGE ISN'T THAT BIG A DEAL FOR ME.

I mean, I hope I'm eventually with someone who I really love, want to be with for the rest of my life. When you're with a girl and you're doing things and you're into each other and feeling the love, I don't know why you need to put a label on it. Either you're with someone or you're not. I mean, when's the clear line before you're considered someone's girlfriend or boyfriend? There isn't. You just kind of ease into it. It should happen

I WANT TO DO MY PART TO KEEP THE BADASS LINE GOING.

naturally. No amount of calling it something is going to make it something if it's not something already.

That said, I definitely want to have kids someday. I want a little me. Definitely. I want a legacy. I want a son so bad, so I can continue myself through my son. I want my son to be totally badass—even more badass than me. And then when he has a son, I want him to be even more badass than his dad! I want to do my part to keep the badass line going.

I MENTIONED TO MY MANAGER THAT I WANTED TO DO SOME MORE ACTING

in TV shows or movies or whatever. I asked if he could get me scripts to read and help me get into that world. So he sent me a script for this horror film called *The Chosen*. If you haven't seen it, it's awesome. It's about a child-stealing demon who attaches itself to this little girl, and we have to battle the evil and send the demon back to hell. I was totally blown away. I knew it could be supercool, and I knew I could act the hell out of this part. So I read for a role, and I got it! It was crazy.

I READ FOR A ROLE, AND I GOT IT! IT WAS CRAZY.

The first time I went onto the set, I felt totally overwhelmed. Making a movie is way different than filming one of our videos. There are lots of people telling you what to do and where to stand. I went from a little camera and just me and Jc in a room, where we're totally in control, to this huge project, where you have to trust in the process! It took time, but I got used to it, and it wound up being a great experience.

of the final film. It's really awesome.

Kian Lawley and Bella Thorne - Snapchat (05/28/15)

AFTER THAT I WAS HOOKED; ACTING WAS LIKE A DRUG,

Beef or pork?

JC: Beef.
KIAN: Beef.

Do you believe in aliens?

KIAN: Yes, but they don't look like us. They look like plants, or floating red balls with strings hanging down, or whatever— but there has to be life outside of Earth.

JC: Most definitely! We have no idea how big the universe is, so there has to be something else out there.

If you were the Presidents of the United States, what would be the first thing you would do?

KIAN: I'd release all the top-secret documents on UFOs and aliens.

JC: I'd change the education system completely. Kids need to learn more street-smart things—like changing a tire, buying a house, paying taxes—and a lot less calculus, which you never use.

If you could have any superpower, what would it be?

JC: I'd want to fly or be able to teleport.

KIAN: Instant regeneration. So I can do crazy stuff, come back to life, and do it again.

What is your favorite non-house pet animal?

JC: Anything that's a baby—baby tiger, baby lion, baby jaguar. They're totally cute. But when they grow older, they get scary.

KIAN: Bobcat or lion. Look at them! They're cats, but they have these big heads. Or a sea horse. Sea horses are awesome.

What's the best way to eat an Oreo?

KIAN: With a fork. Put a fork down the middle of the stuffing so your fingers don't get wet and drop it in a glass of milk.

JC: Put it in milk. No doubt.

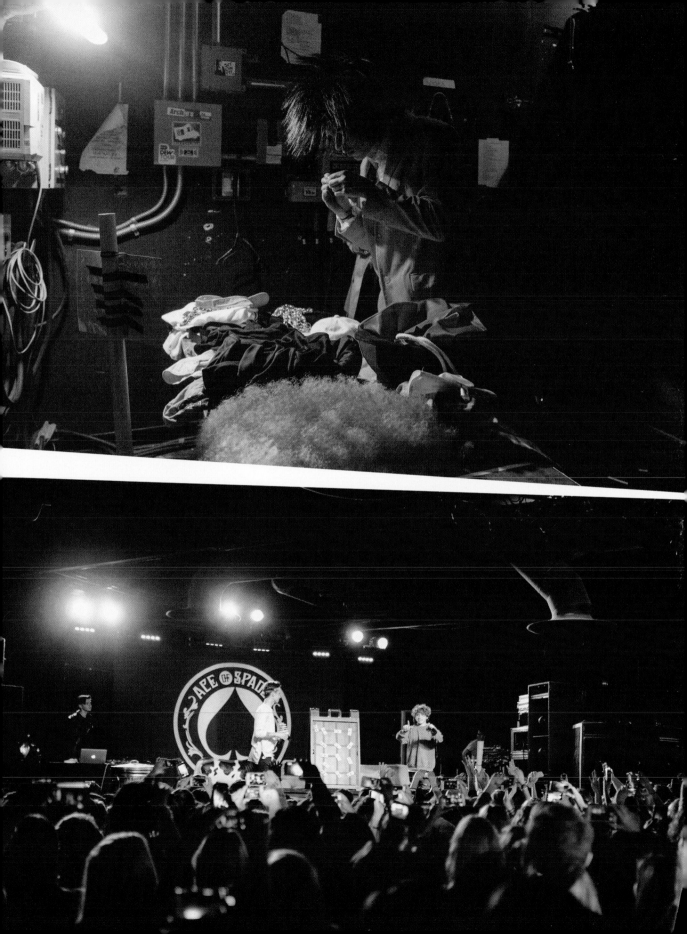

When it comes to toilet paper, are you a crumpler or a folder?

KIAN: Crumpler.

JC: Definitely crumpler.

What's the best way to break up with a girl?

JC: Put it on a banner on a plane. Hey, you asked for the "best" way. Ha-ha. I'm kidding. Definitely just tell her how you feel. Everything works out when you're honest.

KIAN: I'd be up front, no guessing games. Tell her exactly how I feel.

What's your perfect pizza?

KIAN: Pepperoni with garlic crust!

JC: Extra cheese, mushrooms, olives, Canadian bacon, and pepperoni.

OKAY, THIS IS TOTALLY BIZARRE. WE WERE JUST SITTING HERE,

writing our book, when there was a knock at the door. We're friendly guys, so we opened the door, and who do you think we found, standing there? Us! Well, not *us*, because that would be impossible. Duh.

We mean that they were eighty-year-old us's from the future! They must have stolen a time machine or whatever. We didn't ask.

Like we said, we're friendly guys, so we invited them in for pizza, and asked them some questions. We thought you might be interested in the answers.

Hey, eighty-year-old Jc! So, what kind of advice can you give me?

Well, the first thing that pops into my mind is that you're going to hook up with this girl next year. Don't. She's going to completely mess you over.

Wow. Thanks.

But also enjoy yourself. Have fun in your life. Do what you want to do, and be with someone who makes you feel good.

Wow. I'm deep when I'm old.

KIAN: Hey, old me. I see you're totally neck-to-foot tattooed. Nice!

OLD KIAN: Yep. My grandkids are tatted up too!

KIAN: Badass! Nice hovering electric scooter by the way.

OLD KIAN: Yeah, it's pretty cool. I did really well as a director/actor/editor before I retired. I did everything I ever wanted to do—and more.

KIAN: Any advice?

OLD KIAN: Brush your damn teeth. Seriously, we eat all that stupid candy, and now I've got a full set of dentures. You know how hard it is to get romantic with the ladies when you have to pop your teeth out first?

KIAN: Can you tell me, like, what the next lottery numbers will be or who wins the Super Bowl next year?

OLD KIAN: I would, but then the fabric of the universe would tear apart, and we'd all die in a cataclysm of fire and brimstone.

KIAN: Gotcha. So are you and eighty-year-old Jc still friends?

OLD KIAN: Oh hell yeah! We've stayed friends through it all, and it was a hell of a life.

We ate some more pizza and watched some TV, but then we had to ask . . .

JC: So, do you guys want to make a video with us? The whole deal: paintballs, mousetraps, electric shocks?

OLD KIAN & OLD JC: Guys, by the time you reach our age, that stuff doesn't cut it anymore. We play with grenades now and bear traps. But hell yeah! Let's do it anyway.

WE WON'T EVER STOP DOING WHAT WE'RE DOING. . . .